# Top Secret Author Visit

# MOLLY MAC

## by MARTY KELLEY

PICTURE WINDOW BOOKS
a capstone imprint

For Dave Biedrzycki and Russ Cox, two of my favorite authors.
NOW will you guys tell me the big secret to being
a famous author like you?–Marty

Molly Mac is published by
Picture Window Books
A Capstone Imprint
1710 Roe Crest Drive
North Mankato, MN 56003
www.mycapstone.com

Text © 2018 Marty Kelley
Illustrations © 2018 Marty Kelley

Education Consultant: Julie Lemire
Editor: Shelly Lyons
Designer: Ashlee Suker

Library of Congress Cataloging-in-Publication Data
Names: Kelley, Marty, author, illustrator.
Title: Top secret author visit / by Marty Kelley.
Description: North Mankato, Minnesota : Picture Window Books, [2018]
Series: Molly Mac Summary: Excited by the idea that authors actually
get paid real money for writing books, Molly Mac is determined to get
the author visiting her class to reveal the secret to his success, even
going so far as to build a special mind-controlling hat to steal the
secret if necessary–but she is discouraged by what he tells the class.

Identifiers: LCCN 2017040863 (print) LCCN 2017044700 (ebook)
ISBN 9781515823865 (hardcover)
ISBN 9871515823902 (paperback)
ISBN 9781515823940 (eBook PDF)

Subjects: LCSH: Authors–Juvenile fiction. Authorship–Juvenile fiction.
Success–Juvenile fiction. Elementary schools–Juvenile fiction. CYAC:
Authors–Fiction. Authorship–Fiction. Success–Fiction. Schools–Fiction.
Classification: LCC PZ7.K28172 (ebook)
LCC PZ7.K28172 Tq 2018 (print)   DDC [E]–dc23

LC record available at https://lccn.loc.gov/2017040863

# ★ Table of Contents ★

# All About Me!

A picture of me!

Name: Molly Mac

People in my family:
Mom
Dad
Drooly baby brother Alex

My best friend: KAYLEY!!!!

I really like: Crunchy delicious tacos! But not if they have tomatoes on them. Yuck! They are squirty and wet.

When I grow up I want to be: An artist. And a famous animal trainer. And a professional taco taster. And a teacher. And a super hero. And a lunch lady. And a pirate!

My special memory: Kayley and I camped in my yard. We made s'mores with cheese. They were surprisingly un-delicious.

## Chapter 1

# Speed-Reading Stinker

**Ffffp. Ffffp. Ffffp. Ffffp. Ffffp. Ffffp. Ffffp. Ffffp.**

Molly Mac flipped through the pages of her book during quiet reading time.

Kayley looked over at her. "What are you doing, Molly?" she whispered.

"Speed reading," Molly whispered back.

"Whoa," Kayley gasped. "Can you really read that fast?"

"Not exactly," Molly said. "I just learned about speed reading. I'm still in the development stage."

"But why do you want to read so fast?" Kayley asked.

Molly held up her book. "Because this book really stinks."

"Why don't you just stop reading it and get another book?" Kayley asked.

"If you start a book, you have to finish it, no matter how bad it is," Molly explained. "I think it's a law."

Kayley shook her head. "I don't think so," she said.

Mr. Rose stood up and walked over to his large bookshelf. "OK, class," he announced. "Please close your books. I have a fun new project to tell you about."

"Does this new project involve glitter?" Molly asked. "Because I have been banned from using glitter at my house until I'm at least fifty years old."

"No glitter," Mr. Rose said. "Today we're going to start an author study. We're going to learn all about what it's like to write books for a living."

Molly raised her hand. "Whoa, whoa, whoa, there, Mr. Rose," she said. "You mean that writing books is a job?"

"Yes, of course," said Mr. Rose.

"You mean that authors get paid real, actual money for sitting around writing stories?" Molly asked.

"Of course," said Mr. Rose. "Some popular authors get paid a lot of money to write books."

Molly held up the book she was reading. "Even stinkers like this one?" she asked.

Mr. Rose cleared his throat. "I suppose," he said.

A wide smile spread across Molly's face. She took out her sketchbook.

"Do I even want to know what you're smiling about?" asked Kayley.

"Probably not," Molly said.

## Chapter 2

# Super Soft Napkin Pajamas

**Riiiiiiing!**

At recess, Molly and Kayley ran across the playground to their secret snack spot. When they got there, Molly Mac took her sketchbook out of her backpack. She opened it up and started writing.

"Don't you have a snack?" asked Kayley. She opened up her lunch box. She took out a bag of baby carrots, two cookies, and some cheese. "I'll share my snack with you, if you need one."

Molly shook her head. "No, thanks," she said. "I have a snack. I'm just too busy to eat."

Kayley's eyes grew wide. "Too busy to *eat*?" She gasped. "There's no such thing."

"Didn't you hear what Mr. Rose said?" Molly asked. "Authors get paid to sit around writing books. Even stinker books! I bet they never even have to get out of their pajamas!"

Molly leaned over her sketchbook and started writing again.

"So are you working on writing a book?" Kayley asked.

Molly held up a finger. "Shhhh," she whispered. "I'm concentrating."

Kayley ate her snack while Molly wrote.

Soon, Molly smacked her pencil down. "Done!" she announced.

"I didn't know it took that long to write a book," Kayley asked.

Molly shook her head. "It's not a book. First things first. This is a list of things I'm going to get *after* I write a book and get paid a lot of money."

Molly showed the list to Kayley.

Kayley put down her bag of carrots and took the list from Molly.

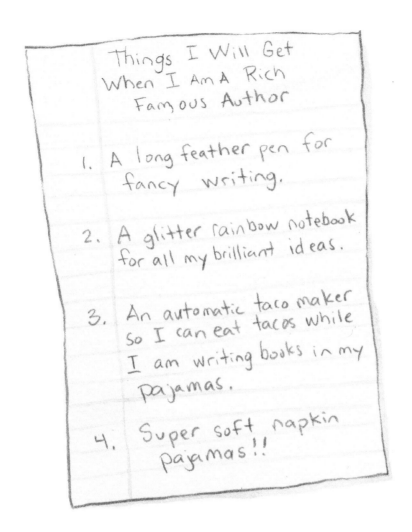

Things I Will Get
When I Am A Rich
Famous Author

1. A long feather pen for fancy writing.

2. A glitter rainbow notebook for all my brilliant ideas.

3. An automatic taco maker so I can eat tacos while I am writing books in my pajamas.

4. Super soft, napkin pajamas!!

"Napkin pajamas?" asked Kayley.

Molly shrugged. "Tacos can get messy," she said.

"Good thinking!" Kayley said. "So what is your book going to be about?"

Molly smiled. "I already have my first brilliant idea! I'm going to write a story about a girl who goes into a house where three bears live."

Kayley frowned. "I think that's already a story," she said.

"OK," Molly said. "Then I'll write a story about a girl who lives with her wicked stepmother and stepsisters who don't let her go to the ball."

Kayley shook her head. "That's already a story too," she replied. "I think you have to come up with your own idea."

Molly tapped
her pencil on her
sketchbook. "Well, how
about a story about a kid
who climbs up a huge
beanstalk and meets a
giant?" she asked.

Kayley shook her head again. "Sorry,
Molly," she said. "That's already a story too."

Molly closed her sketchbook. "Hmmmm,"
she replied. "Writing a book might be harder
than I thought."

## Chapter 3

# A Tasty Science Mystery

**BANG!**

That afternoon, Molly burst through the door of her house. Mom was sitting on the couch reading a book to Alex.

"Hi, Mom!" she said. "Hi, Alex! I'm going to be a famous author with taco-proof pajamas and a fancy feather pen. But other authors have already stolen all the best ideas for stories. Now my brain is empty, and I won't be able to buy a rainbow notebook for all my ideas. What can I write about so my book won't be a stinker?"

Alex smiled and gurgled and chewed on a page in the book.

Mom closed the book she was reading with Alex. "What are you talking about, Molly?" she asked.

Molly sat on the couch with Mom and Alex. "We're starting an author study in school," Molly said. "Mr. Rose told us that people write books for a job! Did you know that?"

Mom nodded. "Of course," she replied.

"Why didn't anybody inform me of this?" Molly asked.

Mom laughed. "Molly, I write stories for the newspaper for a job," she said.

Molly patted Mom's shoulder. "Yeah, but newspapers are boring," she said. "I'm talking about writing something that people actually want to read. Also, Mr. Rose said that some authors are rich and famous. I don't think you qualify."

Mom laughed again. "Most authors are not famous," she explained. "And very few are rich. And my stories for the newspaper are *not* boring, young lady."

"Agree to disagree," Molly said. "But I am going to be a rich, famous, non-boring author with napkin pajamas. I just don't know what to write about. All the ideas I had at school have already been written. What kind of book will make me rich and famous?"

"Well," Mom said, "I don't think that becoming a writer to get rich is a good idea. Authors write because they love writing."

Alex squealed and grabbed the book out of Mom's hands. He chewed on the cover.

Molly laughed and gently took the book out of his mouth. "Alex loves books that taste good," she said.

Mom laughed too. "Everybody likes different kinds of books," she said. "I guess Alex likes tasty books. I like to read books about science. Dad loves to read mystery stories."

"So I should write a tasty mystery about science?" Molly asked. "I can call it, *Who Stole the Candy-Coated Microscope?* Thanks, Mom!"

Molly hopped off Mom's lap.

"No, Molly, no!" Mom said. "You need to write the kind of book *you* would enjoy. Write about something you love."

**"Ahhhhh!"** Molly nodded. "That's a good idea. A tasty science mystery sounded like a stinker."

Molly grabbed her backpack. "I'll write about something I love. If you need me, I'll be upstairs writing my new book about hot fudge and tacos and unicorns and pirates!"

## Chapter 4

# Taco Pirates & Hot Fudge Unicorns

**Knock! Knock! Knock!**

The next day at school, Molly Mac knocked on Mr. Rose's desk.

Mr. Rose smiled at Molly. "I keep telling you, Molly. You don't have to knock. I'm sitting right here. What can I do for you this morning?"

Molly held up a few pieces of paper that were stapled together. "I have a special announcement to make to the class before school," she said. "Would that be OK?"

Mr. Rose took a sip of coffee. "What is your announcement about?" he asked.

"It's about an amazing book!" Molly said.

Mr. Rose nodded. "That sounds great," he replied.

Mr. Rose clapped his hands. "Good morning, class," he said.

Everybody stopped talking. "Good morning, Mr. Rose!" they sang.

"Molly Mac has an announcement to make this morning," said Mr. Rose. "Please give her your attention."

Molly waved her stapled papers over her head. "Behold!" she said. "This is the most amazing book ever written!"

"Is it *The Very Happy Puppy*?" asked Kahil. "That's my favorite book."

"I love the book, *The Unicorn Song*!" said Scott.

"My favorite book is *Henry Hikes a Hill*!" said Ryan.

Molly waved her papers again. "Hello?" she said. "We are talking about my book here. Not *Hiking Henry*."

"I went hiking one time," said Nichole. "But I got a blister. My dad had to carry me on his back."

"My dad's back is hairy," said Joe. "At the beach, he looks like a gorilla in a bathing suit."

Everybody started laughing.

Molly looked over at Mr. Rose. "Is it always this hard to talk to them?" she asked.

Mr. Rose smiled and took a long sip of coffee. "Usually it's harder," he said. He clapped his hands and asked the class to listen to Molly.

"Thank you, Mr. Rose," said Molly. She held up the papers. "Let's try to focus. Last night I wrote the greatest book in the world. It's called *The Taco Pirates vs. the Hot Fudge Unicorns*."

"Ohhhh," Mr. Rose said. "Would you like to read it to the class?"

"Read it to them?" Molly asked. "No way. I want to sell it to them. I'm going to be a rich, famous author!" She held the papers up again. "Who would like to give me a million dollars for this amazing book?"

"Uhhhh, Molly?" Mr. Rose said. "You can't—"

"I only like books about hiking," Ryan interrupted.

"I only like books about puppies," said Kahil.

"I only like books about cheeseburgers," said Ash.

"But I wrote about what I love!" Molly said. "That means that everybody will want to buy my book."

"No, Molly," Mr. Rose said. "First of all, you can't sell things that you make in school."

"Lunchlady Deb makes food and sells it," Molly said.

Mr. Rose sighed. "That's because she has her Lunchlady License. And even if you could sell your book, everybody likes different books."

"So how in the world do authors know what to write about?" Molly asked.

"I'm glad you asked that, Molly," said Mr. Rose. "I have a very special announcement this morning too."

Mr. Rose smiled and held up two books.

Molly's eyes grew wide.

"David Cox, the author of *Faraway Dragons* and *Pirate Alert*, is going to visit our school! He's going to tell us all about being an author! Before he arrives, we will read his books. We will also write down questions to ask him."

"Whoa!" Molly gasped. "A real, live author? Now I can find out the secret to being a rich, famous author!"

## Chapter 5

# The Mind-Control Hat

At lunch, Molly Mac plopped down next to Kayley.

Kayley opened her lunch box. "I have a peanut butter and jelly sandwich," she said. "What do you have, Molly?"

"I'm too busy for lunch," Molly said. She took out her sketchbook and a pencil. She started writing.

Kayley's eyes grew wide. "Too busy for *lunch*?!?" she gasped. "There's no such thing."

"I'm working on a top-secret plan," Molly explained.

"This isn't like that plan you made to fill your entire house with vanilla pudding, is it?" Kayley asked. "Because that plan didn't work out too well."

Molly sighed. "No," she said. "This is a plan to get David Cox to teach me the secret to being a rich, famous author."

"Do you really think there's a secret?" Kayley asked.

"There has to be," Molly explained. "Do you know how to do it?"

Kayley shook her head. "No," she replied.

"Neither do I," Molly said. "So it must be a secret."

"If it's a secret, how are you going to get David Cox to tell you?" Kayley asked.

"It's all here in my plan," Molly said. She showed Kayley her sketchbook.

"A mind-control hat?" Kayley asked.

"Yup," Molly told her. She reached into her backpack. "I got everything I need to build it out of the craft box in our classroom. I have paper, tape, glue sticks, markers, yarn, a paper towel tube, and brain probes."

"Brain probes?" asked Kayley. "Those look like pom-poms and pipe cleaners."

"They're top-secret brain probes in disguise," Molly explained. "I'm going to put them on the hat. Then I'll give the hat to David Cox when he comes to our class. With the hat, I will control his brain and make him tell me the secret of how to be a rich, famous author."

Molly started working on the hat.

Kayley took a bite of her sandwich.

"How does the mind-control hat work?" Kayley asked.

Molly held up a piece of yarn. "I attached one end of this to the brain probe. The other end is attached to this remote control." Molly held up the paper towel tube. It had the words *On* and *Off* written on it. There was a small paper cup glued into one end of the tube. "After David Cox puts the hat on, I will push the *On* button. Then I will control David Cox's brain. When I talk into the microphone, he will have to do anything I tell him to do."

Kayley took another bite of her sandwich. "Are you sure this is going to work?" she asked.

Molly shrugged her shoulders. "Of course it will," she said. "It's science. It has to work."

"I don't know about this, Molly," Kayley said. "What if something goes wrong?"

Molly thought for a minute. "You're right!" she said. She tapped her finger on the mind-control hat. "We need to test this thing!"

## Chapter 6

# Are These Brain Probes Working?

After lunch, Molly and Kayley ran across the playground. Molly was waving her new mind-control hat over her head. "Tori!" she yelled. "Hey, Tori! Tori! Tori!"

They ran up to Tori, who was jumping rope with Ash.

"Tori!" Molly panted. "I need to find out if the brain probes on my mind-control hat work. Put this on!" Molly held the hat out to Tori.

Tori looked at the hat and raised her eyebrow. "Brain probes? Mind-control hat?" she asked. "This isn't like the anti-gravity belt you made that ruined my shirt, is it?"

Molly shook her head. "No, no, no,"
she said. "This is totally different. I built this
mind-control hat so I can give it to David Cox.
It will make him tell me the secret of being a
famous writer so I can get an automatic taco
maker and taco-proof pajamas. I just need to
make sure this hat works."

Molly wiggled the hat in front of Tori.
"Put it on! Put it on!" she said.

Tori took the hat and placed it gently on her head.

Molly held up the paper towel tube and pushed the *On* button. "Beep!" she said.

"You have to say 'Beep'?" asked Kayley.

"It's not finished," Molly explained. She held the tube up to her mouth and spoke quietly into the cup. "Tori, you are under my control."

Tori's eyes grew wide. Her arms lifted in front of her and hung in the air. "Yes, Master," she said slowly. "I am under your control."

Molly, Kayley, and Ash gasped.

"It works!" Molly cried.

"I can't believe it," Kayley said.

Molly held the cup up to her mouth again. "Jump in the air," she said.

Tori jumped in the air.

"Whoa!" Ash said. "That's amazing!" She leaned over the cup and said, "Go get me a cheeseburger!"

"Yes, Master," said Tori. She turned toward the school and took two slow zombie steps.

Then she exploded into laughter. **"Hahaha!"** she laughed. "I was tricking you, Molly!"

Molly groaned. "You weren't really under my control?"

"Nope!" Tori said. "I was just kidding around."

"So I guess I'm not going to get that cheeseburger." Ash sighed.

"And I'm not going to get that secret," Molly said. She lifted the hat off Tori's head. "I have got to make this thing work."

# Chapter 7

# The Big Secret

On Monday morning, Molly Mac sat at her desk in class. She had a colorful band of paper wrapped around her head. It was decorated with dragons and pirates and the words *David Cox Rocks*.

Kayley sat down next to her and smiled. "I like your hat, Molly," she said. "It looks very professional."

Molly sighed. "It's all that's left of my mind-control hat," she said. "This weekend, I was trying to tune up the brain probes and boost their power. I tried adding batteries, but that didn't work. I tried adding a magnifying glass, but that didn't work, either. I even rubbed one of my chewy vitamins on it. That made a mess. Then I tested the hat on baby Alex, but he drooled all over it and ruined it. I used some leftover parts to make this new hat. I thought I would wear this fancy new hat so David Cox will notice me and tell me the big secret."

Kayley nodded her head.

Just then, Mr. Rose stepped through the classroom door. "Ladies and gentlemen!" he announced. "May I have your attention, please?"

Everybody looked up at Mr. Rose.

"I am thrilled to introduce you to . . . David Cox!" Mr. Rose sang. He held his arms out toward the door.

A short, smiling man stepped through the

door and waved. He was carrying a bag.

"Good morning!" he said.

"Good morning, David Cox!" cheered the class.

David Cox walked to the front of the room and put his bag on Mr. Rose's desk.

"I sort of thought he would look more famous," Molly whispered.

"How do you look famous?" asked Kayley.

Molly shrugged. "You know . . . maybe he could wear sunglasses. Or a scarf."

David Cox told the class what it was like to be an author. He explained that he made a lot of mistakes and had to write some of his stories over and over and over again. He said that sometimes he got stuck and didn't know what to write about. He told them that it took him a very long time to write the words for his books, even though the books were very short.

He reached into his bag and took out a huge pile of papers. "This is how much writing I had to do before I was happy with the words for *Faraway Dragons*!" he said.

"Whoa!" Molly gasped.

When David Cox was done telling the class about making books, he asked if anybody had questions.

Everybody's hands shot into the air.

"How many cheeseburgers can you fit in your mouth at once?" asked Ash.

"Do all wrestlers drive red trucks?" asked Kahil.

"When I eat ice cream too fast, why does my brain hurt?" asked Kayley.

Mr. Rose stood up. "How about if we ask David Cox questions about writing," he suggested.

Molly shot her hand into the air. "Oh, oh, oh, oh!! Me, me, mememe!"

David Cox laughed and pointed to Molly. "Yes. The lady with the lovely hat."

Molly smiled. "I really, really want to be a rich, famous author just like you. But I had some trouble making my mind-control hat, so can you just tell us what the big secret is?"

"What big secret?" asked David Cox.

"The secret to being a rich, famous author!" Molly said.

"Well, I'm not rich," David Cox replied. "But I can show you the secret to being a good writer."

Molly's eyes grew wide. She rubbed her hands together.

David Cox held up the pile of papers he had already shown them. "This is the secret," he announced.

"A huge pile of mistakes?" Molly asked. "That's not a secret. That's a mess."

"It is!" David Cox said. "But it's also the secret. I learn from my mistakes, and I keep writing and writing and writing."

Molly sighed and slumped back in her seat. "That's it?" she moaned. "I thought that maybe there was some kind of top-secret author trick. Like maybe you have a robot that writes stories for you while you sit around in your pajamas eating tacos all day."

"Sorry," David Cox said. "No secrets. Just practice and hard work. Did you have to work hard to make that beautiful hat you are wearing?"

Molly nodded. "Yeah!" she said. "It was really, really hard to draw this big dragon. I had to draw it and erase it so many times that my hand got sore."

"See?" David Cox said. "You did your work over and over and over until you were happy with it. That's what I do with my writing. Maybe you could be an illustrator and draw pictures to go in books. That would be a great job for a wonderful artist like you."

Molly sat up and grabbed her desk. "You mean people get paid to sit around in their taco-proof napkin pajamas and draw pictures?" she cried.

"They do," laughed David Cox. "I have a lot of friends who are wonderful illustrators. It's a very fun job. Does anyone else have any questions?"

Molly grabbed her sketchbook, opened it, and started drawing a picture of a taco pirate.

Kayley leaned over. "Do I even want to know what you're doing right now, Molly?" she asked.

"Probably not," Molly told her.

# All About Me!

A picture of me!

Name:
Marty Kelley

People in my family:
My lovely wife, Kerri
My amazing son, Alex
My terrific daughter, Tori

I really like: Pizza! And hiking in the woods.
And being with my friends. And reading. And
making music. And traveling with my family.

When I grow up I want to be:
A rock star drummer!

My special memory:
Sitting on the couch with my kids
and reading a huge pile of books
together.

Find more at my website: www.martykelley.com

# ≡ MORE ≡

# MOLLY MAC

Meet Molly Mac, the curious
girl who is always onto
something. She's a whirlwind
full of questions, and she's
out to find the answers!

**MOLLY MAC**

≥ The Best Friend Bandit ≤
by MARTY KELLEY

**MOLLY MAC**

≥ Tooth Fairy Trouble ≤
by MARTY KELLEY

**MOLLY MAC**

≥ Lucky Break ≤
by MARTY KELLEY

# THE FUN DOESN'T STOP HERE!

Discover more at
www.capstonekids.com

★ Videos & Contests
★ Games & Puzzles
★ Friends & Favorites
☆ Authors & Illustrators